HIAWATHA AND THE PEACEMAKER

WORDS BY ROBBIE ROBERTSON
PICTURES BY DAVID SHANNON

ABRAMS BOOKS FOR YOUNG READERS
NEW YORK

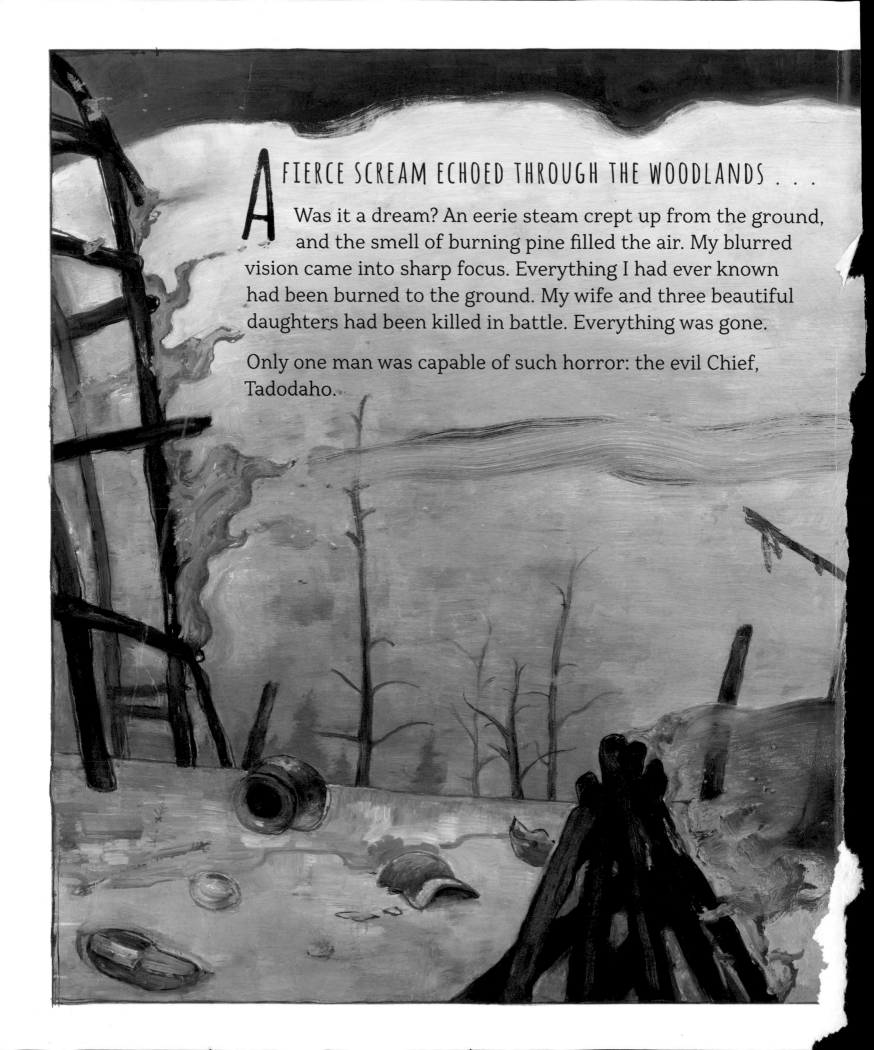

A FIERCE SCREAM ECHOED THROUGH THE WOODLANDS . . .

Was it a dream? An eerie steam crept up from the ground, and the smell of burning pine filled the air. My blurred vision came into sharp focus. Everything I had ever known had been burned to the ground. My wife and three beautiful daughters had been killed in battle. Everything was gone.

Only one man was capable of such horror: the evil Chief, Tadodaho.

I took shelter up the river. I had only a small fire and a place to sleep. I dressed my wounds with leaves I gathered from the bush. Days, then weeks, went by. Consumed by anger and hunger and sleeplessness, I could think only of revenge.

The sun rose early one morning and burned the mist off the river. It was as if a path had been cleared for what happened next. A blinding reflection came off the water, and from it a man paddled gently toward me. As he reached the shore, I realized the reflection was caused by the sun hitting his hand-carved white stone canoe.

"Who are you? Why have you come here?" I asked. He answered only with a smile, and handed me a string of wampum shells as an offering. We stood quietly, observing each other, and then he spoke softly, stumbling over his words. "I–I–I know of your pain. I know of your loss. I carry a message of healing. I h–h–have come to tell you of the Great Law: Fighting among our people must stop. We must come together as one body, one mind, and one heart. Peace, power, and righteousness shall be the new way."

I considered his words, but didn't believe him.
Our people governed only through fear. I had never
thought peace among our tribes was a possibility.

The man spoke again. "T–t–travel with me to the land
of the Mohawk, and let us spread the good word. As
you can hear, my voice is quiet and my words difficult
to understand. I know that you speak with power and
confidence and that your voice carries straight to the
heart. I need your help, my friend. I need you to help
me carry this message."

I agreed to travel with him and help carry his message.

AND SO I, HIAWATHA, CAME TO TELL THE STORY OF THE GREAT PEACEMAKER.

I stared at his stone canoe, bewildered by its ability to float. But we paddled off, and with every impossible moment that the canoe glided across the water, I became more of a believer. When we arrived at the land of my people, the Mohawk, we were greeted warmly. The Chief and the Elders were summoned, and we gathered in a circle. A few Clan Mothers looked on with curiosity and concern.

The Peacemaker closed his eyes and placed his hand on my back. Somehow he had the power to move his message through me. I began to speak his words. "Peace, power, and righteousness shall be the new way," I said. "We must join together. All nations will become *one family*. Our people shall have *one body, one mind, and one heart*. This is the message of the Great Law."

The Clan Mothers nodded in agreement, and a sense of relief spread over me. But then the War Chief spoke. "We respect your message, but we cannot join you," he said. "How can we know if your words are true? Tadodaho is too strong, too violent. Our people must be prepared to fight."

The Peacemaker quietly stuttered, "The Great Law is more powerful than any one man. We will return with proof that our nations *can* join together."

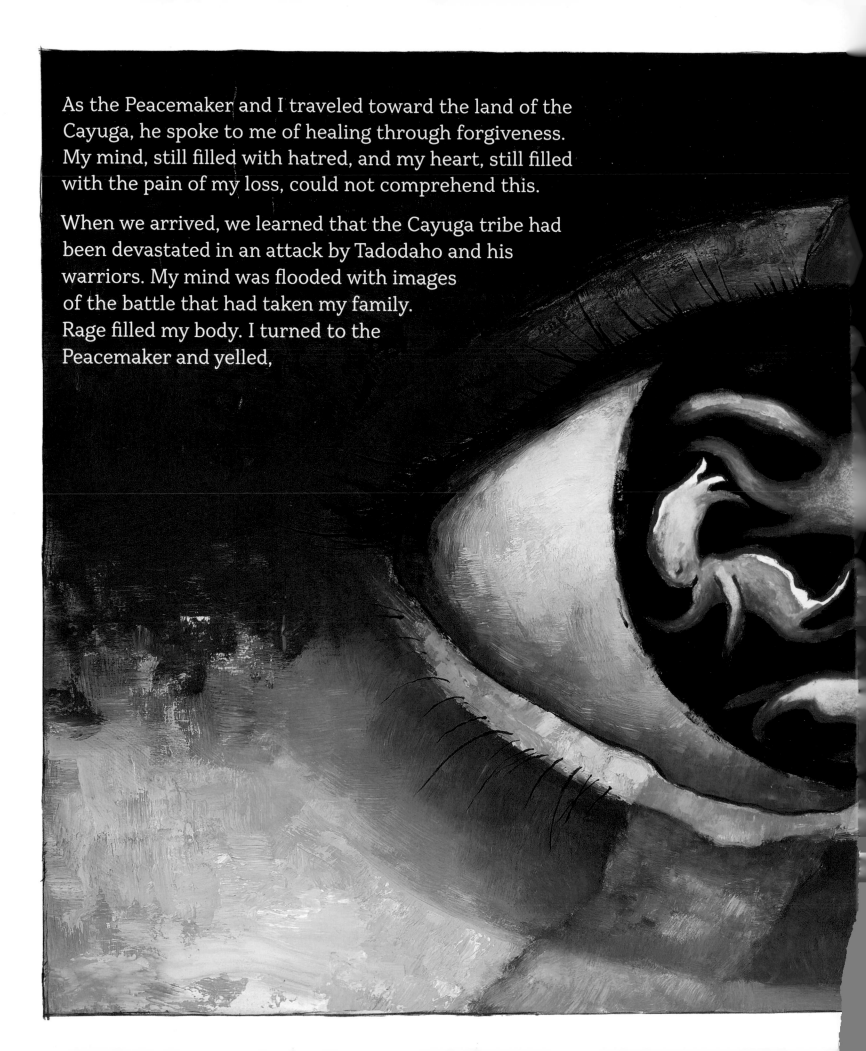

As the Peacemaker and I traveled toward the land of the Cayuga, he spoke to me of healing through forgiveness. My mind, still filled with hatred, and my heart, still filled with the pain of my loss, could not comprehend this.

When we arrived, we learned that the Cayuga tribe had been devastated in an attack by Tadodaho and his warriors. My mind was flooded with images of the battle that had taken my family. Rage filled my body. I turned to the Peacemaker and yelled,

"WE WILL NEVER BE FREE!"

In an attempt to soothe me, the Peacemaker asked me to sit with him and the Cayuga council. He looked deep into my eyes as he spoke to the people. "I do not see defeat," he said. "What I see is a passage—a passage to a new way of life. Join me, and together we can spread peace rather than war, love rather than hate, unity rather than fear."

The Peacemaker placed his fist over his heart. A feeling of strength and trust ran down my spine. With new hope, we headed toward the Great Hill to see the Seneca people. The Cayuga Chief followed us in his canoe.

TOGETHER WE PADDLED AS ONE NATION.

We were met by fifteen armed braves. For the first time, the Peacemaker showed signs of worry. We were surrounded by warriors and led to the center of the Seneca village. The Seneca Chief approached the circle, and the guards closed in on us. With a wave of his hand, the warriors lifted their spears. But then he nodded, and the guards drove their spears deep into the dirt. The Seneca Chief sat down and told us that the wind had carried our message from the land of the Cayuga. The Seneca people wanted to learn about the Peacemaker and the Great Law.

"We will all perish if we continue this violence. A change must come, and the time is now. Alone, we will be broken," I said, "but together we are more powerful than the greatest warrior."

The Seneca Chief trailed us in his canoe,

AND TOGETHER WE RODE AS TWO NATIONS.

Guided by the moon, we trekked through the forest to the land of the Oneida people. We were halfway to the camp when the snap of a stick was heard through the trees. Suddenly, the earth beneath our feet gave way. We hit the ground and were then engulfed by a giant net.

The Oneida Chief stood towering over us. "I've spared your life," he declared. "Why would two chiefs and two strangers be so foolish as to enter our territory in the darkness?" His men dragged us through the dirt and bound our hands.

The Peacemaker explained that we had joined the Cayuga and Seneca nations in the name of peace, but his words had no power with the Oneida. Then the Peacemaker turned to me and said, "Tell your story, Hiawatha. Tell us of your great loss."

I spoke of my pain and of my hatred for Tadodaho. I told the Oneida that my wife and three daughters had been killed by the violent world we had created. But as I spoke, I felt something come over me: *Forgiveness.* I had not been able to save my family, but on this journey I had been able to forgive *myself.* I began to understand the meaning of the Great Law, and I turned to the Peacemaker and placed my fist over my heart. With a knowing nod, he smiled.

A warrior approached, and he untied all of us, one by one.

Rather than feel the anger that had consumed me, I now remembered the joy of my family. I was joined by the Cayuga Chief, the Seneca Chief, the Peacemaker, and, lastly, the Oneida Chief.

TOGETHER WE TRAVELED AS THREE NATIONS.

The time had come to return to the Mohawk people with proof of our message. When we arrived, they were impressed to see the three Chiefs with us. The Clan Mothers had a glowing look of approval.

But the Mohawk Chief told us that word of our mission had traveled to Tadodaho. "His evil is too great," he said. "Your message will only bring harm to our people."

Angered by his lack of faith, the Oneida Chief pressed the sharpened tip of his staff under the chin of the Mohawk Chief.

"We no longer use violence," said the Peacemaker as he reached out and lowered the staff from under the Chief's chin.

The Peacemaker led us to the tallest oak that towered over the Mohawk River. "I will climb this tree," he said, "and your men shall cut it down. But I will not perish. The river will catch my body and carry it to safety. Then you will know that my words are true."

The men chopped down the massive tree. It crashed into the icy waters, and the Peacemaker vanished.

I stood silent, stunned by this foolish stunt. I feared the Peacemaker had sacrificed himself at a critical point in our journey.

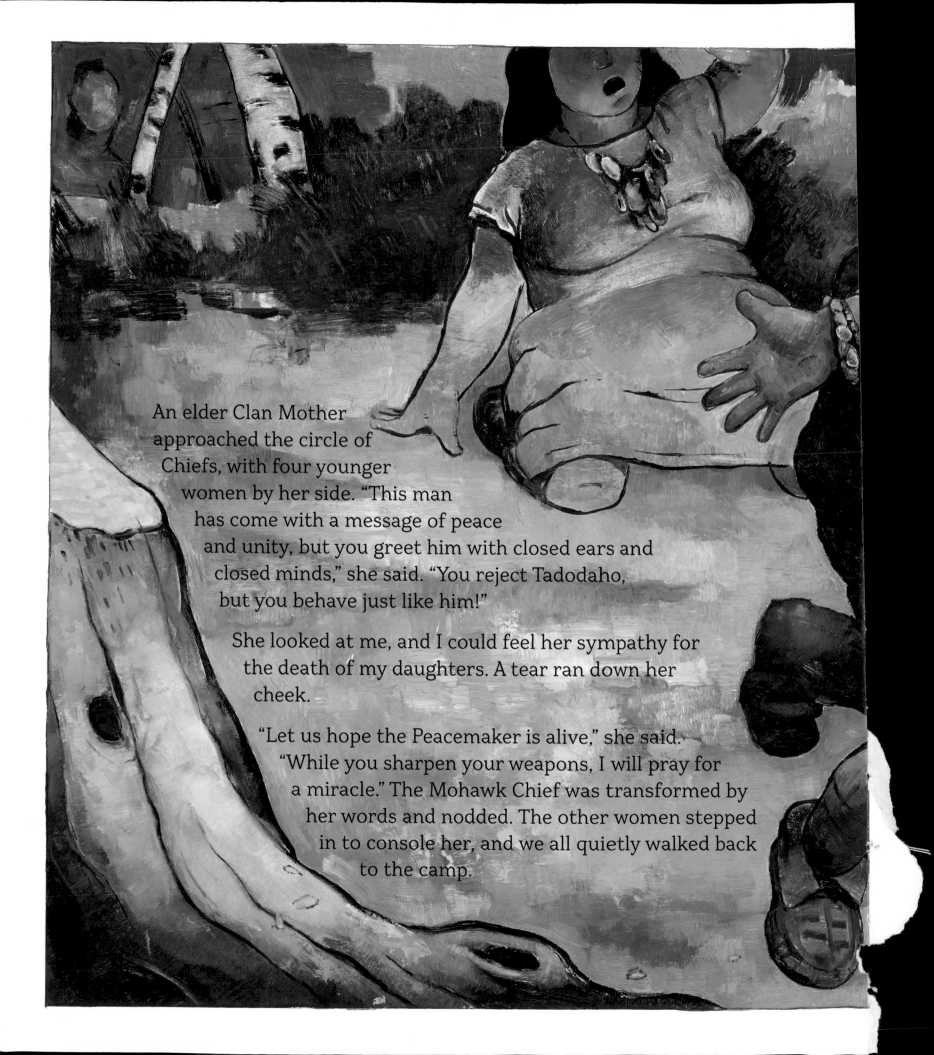

An elder Clan Mother
approached the circle of
Chiefs, with four younger
women by her side. "This man
has come with a message of peace
and unity, but you greet him with closed ears and
closed minds," she said. "You reject Tadodaho,
but you behave just like him!"

She looked at me, and I could feel her sympathy for
the death of my daughters. A tear ran down her
cheek.

"Let us hope the Peacemaker is alive," she said.
"While you sharpen your weapons, I will pray for
a miracle." The Mohawk Chief was transformed by
her words and nodded. The other women stepped
in to console her, and we all quietly walked back
to the camp.

When we arose in the morning, smoke from the river's edge caught our attention. We hurried down to find the Peacemaker sitting by a fire, patiently waiting for us. The elder Clan Mother draped a blanket across his shoulders, and relief spread among us. Filled with emotion, the Mohawk Chief agreed to follow us in his canoe to the land of the Onondaga to confront Chief Tadodaho.

TOGETHER WE PADDLED AS FOUR NATIONS.

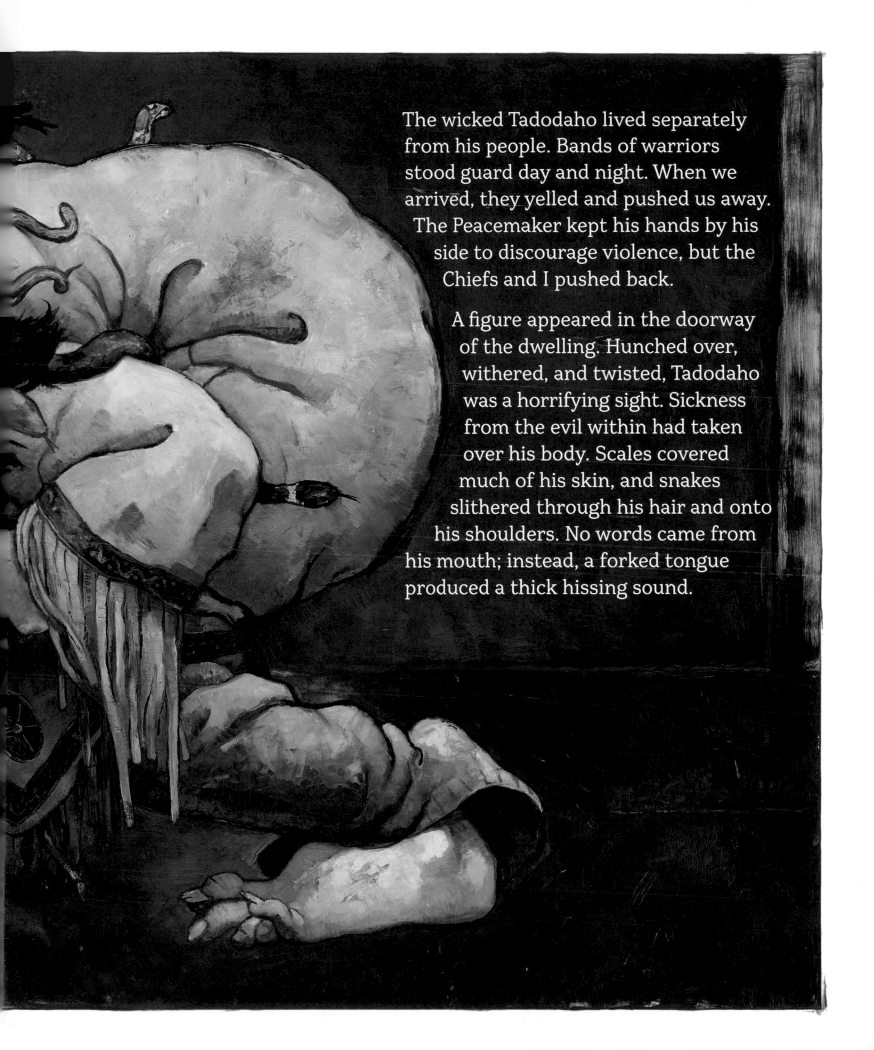

The wicked Tadodaho lived separately from his people. Bands of warriors stood guard day and night. When we arrived, they yelled and pushed us away. The Peacemaker kept his hands by his side to discourage violence, but the Chiefs and I pushed back.

A figure appeared in the doorway of the dwelling. Hunched over, withered, and twisted, Tadodaho was a horrifying sight. Sickness from the evil within had taken over his body. Scales covered much of his skin, and snakes slithered through his hair and onto his shoulders. No words came from his mouth; instead, a forked tongue produced a thick hissing sound.

My anger returned, and I wanted to destroy Tadodaho. The Chiefs continued to push against the warriors. The fighting grew . . . until something unexpected happened.

A soft, haunting melody of purity and truth came floating through the air. Spellbound, all lowered their weapons.

The hymn was coming from the lips of the Peacemaker. His melody had stopped the fighting. As the song drifted through the air, the moon crossed in front of the sun, darkening the blue sky. This miracle stunned the warriors, and they pulled back in fear. But the rest of us were enchanted by the glory of the hymn, and we joined in singing.

Tadodaho cursed the sky, waving his scepter and showing no sign of fear.

As the Peacemaker finished his singing, the moon passed, revealing the sun again, more beautiful than before. The Peacemaker asked me to make medicine for Tadodaho's sickness. He said that where there is darkness, we must bring light, and that it is by forgiving that we are set free.

I gathered roots and herbs for the medicine. But how could I help heal a man who had brought me such misery? How could I forgive him?

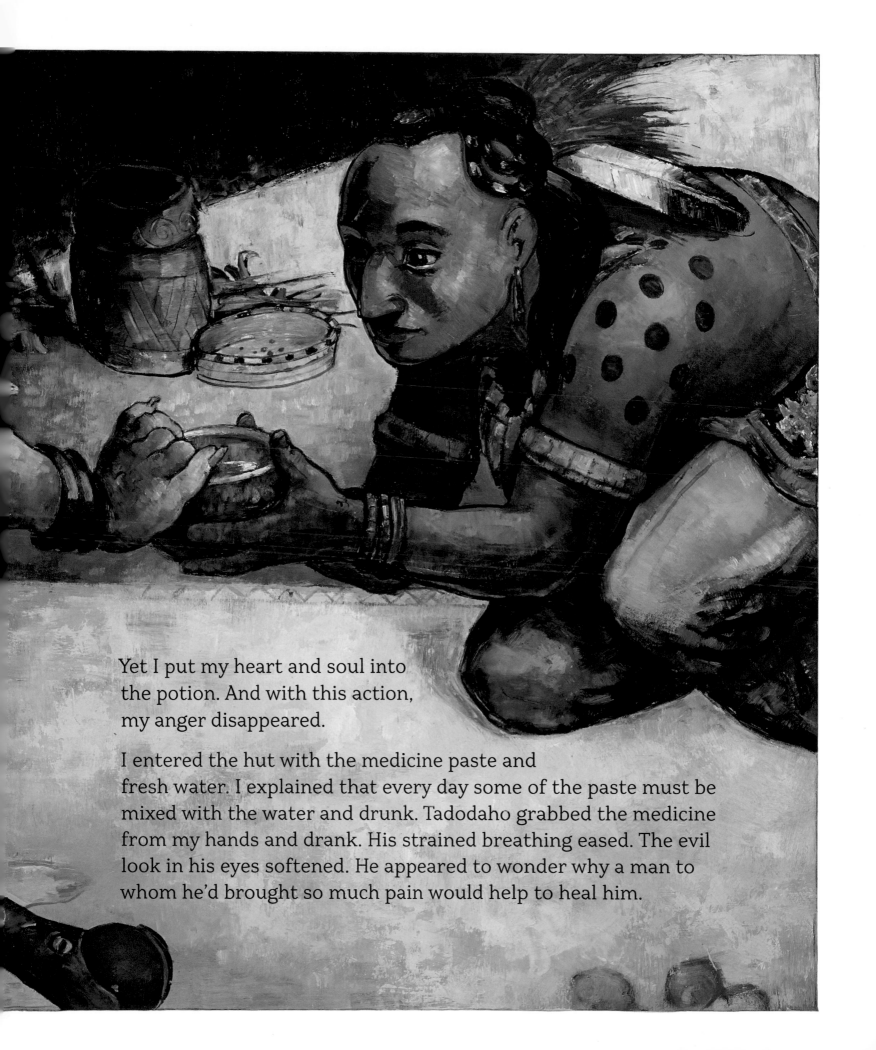

Yet I put my heart and soul into
the potion. And with this action,
my anger disappeared.

I entered the hut with the medicine paste and
fresh water. I explained that every day some of the paste must be
mixed with the water and drunk. Tadodaho grabbed the medicine
from my hands and drank. His strained breathing eased. The evil
look in his eyes softened. He appeared to wonder why a man to
whom he'd brought so much pain would help to heal him.

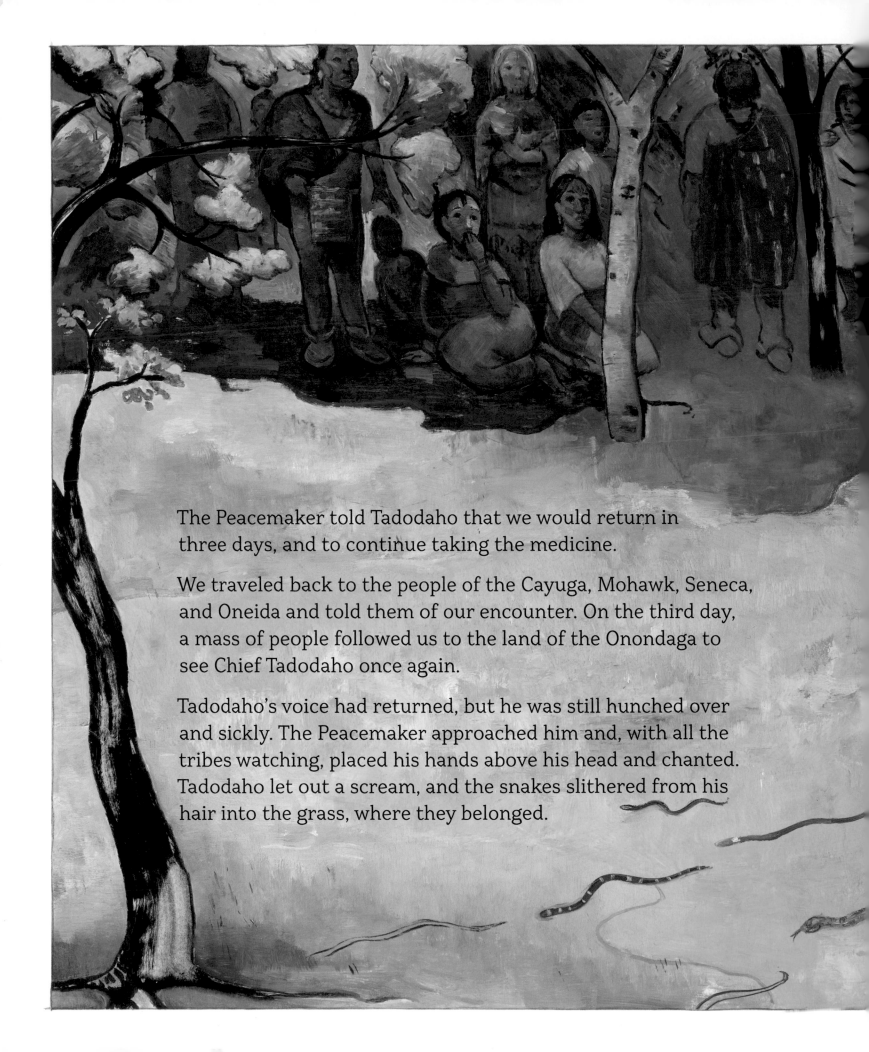

The Peacemaker told Tadodaho that we would return in
three days, and to continue taking the medicine.

We traveled back to the people of the Cayuga, Mohawk, Seneca,
and Oneida and told them of our encounter. On the third day,
a mass of people followed us to the land of the Onondaga to
see Chief Tadodaho once again.

Tadodaho's voice had returned, but he was still hunched over
and sickly. The Peacemaker approached him and, with all the
tribes watching, placed his hands above his head and chanted.
Tadodaho let out a scream, and the snakes slithered from his
hair into the grass, where they belonged.

Everyone followed the Peacemaker to a tall white pine.
He placed his hand on my back, and once again I spoke for him.
"People of all nations must now come together as one. Beneath this tree we shall bury all our weapons of war. This will symbolize the end of our fighting."
The men uprooted the white pine and threw their weapons into the hole.
"Now we will replant this tree, and it shall be called the Tree of Peace."

As I looked at Tadodaho, the scales on his skin began to disappear.

The Peacemaker placed his fist over his heart, and again I spoke. "As Five Nations, we will bring forth peace, power, and righteousness. The women of our tribes shall appoint the Chiefs, and as one people we shall live under the protection of the Great Law. All voices will be heard as we now vote before action is taken."

I looked at Tadodaho, and the once crooked man now stood upright.

"Atop this great white pine shall live an eagle that will look over all Five Nations, and that eagle shall be you, Tadodaho. You will be the great keeper of peace and the protector of all the people."

The men and women of the Mohawk nation began to stomp their feet in unison. Clapping came from the Cayuga, a chant formed between the Onondaga and the Oneida, and the Seneca pounded drums. The rhythm grew louder, in perfect time, and the melody soared through the pines.

I looked over to Tadodaho, but he was gone. A beautiful scream echoed through the woodlands . . .

AND AS FIVE NATIONS, WE LOOKED UP TO SEE AN EAGLE PERCHED ATOP THE TREE OF PEACE.

HISTORICAL NOTE

Hiawatha and the Peacemaker are thought to have lived in the fourteenth century, before Europeans traveled to North America. The Peacemaker, whose birth name was Deganawida, was a spiritual leader who was known for his sacred powers. Historians believe he had a speech impediment, and that he chose Hiawatha to accompany him because Hiawatha was a gifted speaker. The two men journeyed across what is now upper New York State and Ontario and Quebec, Canada, to unite the five nations of the Iroquois people who had been at war: the Cayugas, the Senecas, the Oneidas, the Mohawks, and the Onodagas. Much later, in 1722, the Tuscarora nation joined this united league, and it became the Six Nations Iroquois Confederacy. Officially, it was known as the *Haude-nosaunee*, or People of the Long House. This meant that all Iroquois were one family and could live in peace under one roof.

The Peacemaker's message of the Great Law of Peace pledged peace among the nations by giving each tribe a special role in how the Iroquois governed themselves. Each village and clan would choose a chief to represent it at the council of tribes. All decisions were made by consensus at the council, meaning that all voices had equal importance. Men and women shared power.

It is said that the Great Law of Peace is the oldest participatory democracy on earth and it had much influence on Benjamin Franklin, John Hancock, Thomas Jefferson, and the authors of Constitution of the United States, who also supported self-government and a peaceful union.

To this day, the Six Nations live in unity, harmony, and peace based on the teachings of the Great Law from the Peacemaker and his disciple, Hiawatha.

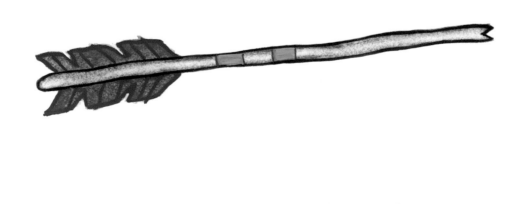

ACKNOWLEDGMENTS

I would like to thank my son, Sebastian Robertson, who inspired me to share this story from my childhood. He connected with this part of our heritage, did all the research, and helped me find the words to make the story come to life for young readers. I am so deeply grateful to and proud of Sebastian for his invaluable contribution to this book.

In honor of the memory and teachings of Chief Jake Thomas (Cayuga) of Six Nations.

Thanks to Yvonne Thomas (Seneca), Chief Roberta Jamieson (Mohawk), and Tom Hill (Seneca) for their knowledge and insights on this project.

With respect and appreciation to Jake Swamp (Mohawk) and Tom Porter (Mohawk).

With acknowledgment to the books *The Legend of the Peacemaker, Part 1* and *The Great Laws of Peace, Part 2* by Jake Thomas, and *White Roots of Peace: Iroquois Book of Life* by Paul Wallace.

Special thanks to Jared Levine, Ryan Harbage, Jim Guerinot, and, of course, Michael Jacobs and the wonderful Tamar Brazis.

When I asked my editor who might be the right illustrator for this book, her response came quickly. She sent me artwork by David Shannon, although she was concerned that he might be unavailable. When I saw Mr. Shannon's work, I found it tremendously impressive. I invited him to my studio so we could meet and at least talk about the project. He graciously obliged, and I told him the story of Hiawatha and the Peacemaker, and played him a song I was recording based on the story. Afterward, he said, "I was coming here to tell you that I wouldn't be able to work on the book, but after hearing this story and this song, I *have* to do it." Needless to say, I was thrilled, and the results are beyond extraordinary. Thank you, David!

AUTHOR'S NOTE

When I was around nine years old, something happened that made a deep impression on my life. My mother and I, who are of Mohawk and Cayuga heritage, were visiting our relatives at Six Nations of the Grand River in southern Ontario, Canada. We would travel from Toronto to the reservation three or four times a year, and it never failed to thrill me.

My cousins, uncles, and aunts were all very gifted. Some had a deep understanding of nature or unusual athletic ability. They didn't climb a tree—they ran up a tree. I broke my arm trying to keep up. But the highlight for me was the music. It seemed that everyone played an instrument, sang, or danced, and I just naturally wanted to be part of that club. I was immediately drawn to the guitar, and pretty soon my relatives started showing me my first chords. Not many things sent chills down my spine like the times we got together and had a down-home, traditional, Six Nations jam session.

One particular day, I experienced another ritual of the Haudenosaunee (Iroquois) Nation that sent chills right through me. After lunch, everybody set off on a walk somewhere. I had no idea where we were going—at that age, tagging along was a specialty of mine.

We ventured about a half mile through "the bush," a nickname for the reserve, and came upon an unusual-looking building. Some neighbors and more of our relatives were hanging around outside, like they were waiting for something special. Kids my age were running around, playing tag, and building little rock sculptures. The grown-ups greeted one another and shared tobacco from little pouches—not so much for smoking as for blessings. This was an extremely different scenario from anything I had experienced back in the city. I didn't understand why we were there, but I could sense a spiritual feeling to the gathering.

A girl in her late teens came out of the building, and said, "He'll be here shortly."

"What is this place?" I asked my mother.

My mother explained that it was a longhouse—a narrow one-room building that traditionally housed Iroquois families.

Moments later, a striking-looking older man with a walking stick appeared out of the bush. He walked through the crowd without making eye contact with anybody and headed straight to the door of the longhouse. Everybody fell quiet as he passed by. I didn't know why everyone acted this way, but one thing was clear: he was certainly revered.

One of my uncles announced, "Come on in. He's going to tell a story now."

My mother took me by the arm and led me inside.

"Who is that man? What's going to happen?" I asked.

She whispered, "He's a very respected elder, a wisdom-keeper who knows the stories and the old ways. Pay attention, and be still."

The kids all gathered close, sitting cross-legged near his feet. He faced the crowd, and spoke in a Native tongue. He said a prayer of gratitude, thanking us all for being together on this beautiful day. As his eyes wandered across the room at the people in attendance, he looked at us kids, and for the first time a slight hint of a smile creased his mouth. He sat down in a large pine chair draped in skins, closed his eyes as if in a trance, and then tapped his walking stick a couple of times on the floor. The Elder began to speak.

"Many hundred years ago in the North Country, an uneasy stillness filled the air. It was as if the wind was holding its breath, and no birds dared to sing. Between the pine forests and the Great Lakes, Mother Nature always made her voice heard, but today, it was quiet, too quiet . . ."

The sound of his voice was mesmerizing. We were spellbound. He told us of the Great Peacemaker and his disciple, Hiawatha. At the end of this incredible story and powerful experience, I said to my mother, "I hope someday when I grow up, I can tell stories like that."

She smiled and patted me on the back and said, "I think you will."

Some years later in school, we were studying Henry Wadsworth Longfellow's poem about Hiawatha. I think I was the only one in the class who knew that Longfellow got Hiawatha mixed up with another Indian. I knew his poem was not about the *real* Hiawatha, whom I had learned about years ago, that day in the longhouse. I didn't say anything. I kept the truth to myself . . . till now.

FOR MY MOTHER, ROSEMARIE MYKE CRYSLER ROBERTSON
—R.R.

FOR HEIDI
—D.S.

The illustrations in this book were painted in oils on hot press illustration boards.

Library of Congress Cataloging-in-Publication Data

Robertson, Robbie, author.
Hiawatha and the Peacemaker / by Robbie Robertson ; illustrated by David Shannon.
pages cm
Summary: Hiawatha, a Mohawk, is plotting revenge for the murder of his wife and
daughters by the evil Onondaga Chief, Tadodaho, when he meets the Great Peacemaker, who
enlists his help in bringing the nations together to share his vision of a new way of life marked
by peace, love, and unity rather than war, hate, and fear. Includes historical notes.
ISBN 978-1-4197-1220-3
[1. Peace—Fiction. 2. Indians of North America—Fiction.
3. Six Nations—History—Fiction.] I. Shannon, David, illustrator. II. Title.
PZ7.1.R635Hi 2015
[Fic]—dc23
2014041310

Printed and bound in China
10 9 8 7 6 5 4 3 2 1

Abrams Books for Young Readers are available at special discounts when purchased
in quantity for premiums and promotions as well as fundraising or educational use. Special editions
can also be created to specification. For details, contact specialsales@abramsbooks.com or the address below.

THE ART OF BOOKS SINCE 1949
115 West 18th Street
New York, NY 10011
www.abramsbooks.com